This book
belongs to

_____

Marvellous Munsch!

A Robert Munsch
Collection

Illustrated by
Michael Martchenko

Scholastic Canada Ltd.
Toronto New York London Auckland Sydney
Mexico City New Delhi Hong Kong Buenos Aires

www.scholastic.ca

The art for this book was painted in watercolour on Crescent illustration board.

Library and Archives Canada Cataloguing in Publication

Munsch, Robert N., 1945-
[Novels. Selections]
Marvellous Munsch : a Robert Munsch collection / Robert
Munsch ; illustrated by Michael Martchenko.

Contents: Down the drain! -- Put me in a book! -- Too much
stuff! -- Moose! -- Give me back my dad!
ISBN 978-1-4431-4863-4 (hardback)

1. Children's stories, Canadian (English). I. Martchenko, Michael, illustrator
II. Munsch, Robert N., 1945- Down the drain! III. Munsch, Robert N., 1945- Put me
in a book! IV. Munsch, Robert N., 1945- Too much stuff! V. Munsch, Robert N.,
1945- Moose! VI Munsch, Robert N., 1945- Give me back my dad! VII. Title.

PS8576.U575A6 2016   jC813'.54   C2016-901218-2

Page 178: Labrador tent photo courtesy of Terry Whey, Goose Bay, Labrador.

6 5 4 3 2 1   Printed in Malaysia 108   16 17 18 19 20

Contents

*To Cheryl Allen,
Rigolet, Labrador.*
—R.M.

GIVE ME BACK MY DAD!

Robert Munsch   Michael Martchenko

One day, Cheryl and her father decided to go ice fishing. They got on the snowmobile, put all their stuff in the sled on the back, and went bouncing over bumps and across lakes until they came to a very good place to fish.

"This place," said Cheryl's father, "is the best place to fish in the whole world. But the fish are smart. You've got to be really smart to catch these fish."

"Phooey!" said Cheryl. "I'm smarter than any fish."

So her father got out an ice drill and drilled an enormous hole. They chopped the ice and drilled some more, and then they were done.

"WOW!" said Cheryl's father. "Really thick ice! Now we can fish!"

He got out a hook and line and bait and said to Cheryl, "You fish down this hole, but be very careful because these fish are smart."

"Phooey!" said Cheryl. "I'm smarter than any fish."

She jigged her line

up and **down** and

    up and **down** and

        up and **down** and

            up and **down**

and said, "I want to catch a fish."

"Be patient," said her dad.

So Cheryl jigged her line

up and **down** and

    up and **down** and

        up and **down** and

            up and **down**

and said, "I want to catch a fish."

Then up out of the hole came a candy bar with a line on it.

"Look at that!" said Cheryl. "It's a candy bar."

Her father yelled,

"DON'T TOUCH THAT!"

But Cheryl grabbed the candy bar and was pulled right down underneath the ice.

Cheryl's father yelled down the hole, **"Give me back my baby!"**

A big fish stuck its head out of the water and said, "We caught this kid fair and square. You can't have her back."

"Grrrrr," said Cheryl's father.

13

Cheryl's father got an idea. He put
a very small piece of bait on a line and
jigged it

UP and *down* and

    UP and *down* and

        UP and *down* and

            UP and *down*

and all of a sudden he pulled up a very
small baby fish.

The big fish stuck its head out of the
water and said, **"Give me back my
baby!"**

"Well," said Cheryl's father, "I'll give you
back YOUR baby if you will give me back
MY baby."

"Grrrrr," said the big fish.

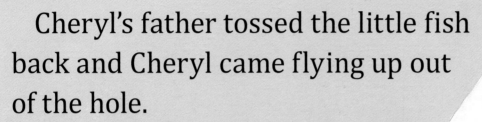

Cheryl's father tossed the little fish back and Cheryl came flying up out of the hole.

She said, "Brrrrrrrrr, it's cold," and right away she started turning into an icicle.

Her father picked her up, ran to shore and got a fire going in the Labrador tent.

Soon Cheryl was warm and dry like a piece of toast.

"Now," said her father, "we are going back out there. Don't pick up anything the fish throw out of the hole. These are smart fish."

"Right!" said Cheryl.

They went back out and Cheryl jigged her line

up and **down** and
   up and **down** and
      up and **down** and
         up and **down**

and said, "I want to catch a fish."

A candy bar with a line on it came up out of the hole.

"Oh no," said Cheryl, "I'm not that dumb."
She jigged her line

up and **down** and
    up and **down** and
        up and **down** and
            up and **down**

and said, "I want to catch a fish."

Up came a bag of popcorn with a line on it.

Cheryl said, "Oh no, I'm not that dumb."
She jigged her line

up and **down** and
    up and **down** and
        up and **down** and
            up and **down**

and said, "I want to catch a fish."

Then up came a television.

"WOW!" said Cheryl. "That looks pretty nice. But I'm not that dumb."

Cheryl jigged her line
up and **down** and
up and **down** and
up and **down** and
up and **down**
and said, "I want to catch a fish."

She waited some more, and up came a $50,000 bill with a line on it.

Her father said, "Fifty thousand dollars!" He grabbed it and got pulled underneath the ice.

"Grrrrr," said Cheryl. She yelled down the hole,

"Give me back my daddy!"

The baby fish stuck its head up out of the water and said, "Hey! We caught him fair and square and you can't have him back."

Cheryl got an idea. She put a huge piece of bait on the line and she jigged it

UP and **down** and

UP and **down** and

UP and **down** and

UP and **down**

and said, "I've got to catch a daddy fish."

All of a sudden a big fish grabbed the bait and Cheryl pulled him in.

The baby fish stuck its head out of the water and said, **"Give me back my daddy!"**

"Well," said Cheryl, "I'll give you back YOUR daddy if you give me back MY daddy."
"Grrrr!" said the little fish.

Cheryl threw the daddy fish back into the water and Cheryl's father came flying up out of the hole. He said, "Brrrrrrrrr, it's cold," and started turning into an icicle.

Cheryl pulled her father to the tent and put wood into the stove till he was warm and dry like a piece of toast.

Then Cheryl said, "Daddy, why did you grab the money? I thought you were smarter than a fish."

"I AM smarter than a fish," said her dad. "And I know that YOU are smarter than any fish, and I knew you would get me out. And I still have the money!"

"Right!" said Cheryl, and they went back to town and bought Cheryl her very own snowmobile.

GIVE ME BACK MY DAD!

Give Me Back My Dad! was written while I was on a trip to Rigolet, Labrador with my son, Andrew. While we were there we went ice fishing with a girl named Cheryl and her father, Roger.

Andrew got a new snowsuit and mukluk sort of boots and I was given a snowsuit and a new parka. They suggested I wear new boots and I said mine were okay, but it was a mistake. Every time I went through the snow I got snow in the top of my boots and eventually my socks got wet. I should have taken their advice!

Next to their fishing cabin they put up a Labrador tent. They make it by cutting down two spruce trees, pounding one into the snow and then lashing the other across the top to an uncut tree. This makes a pole to hang the tent from. They cut spruce branches and make a thick bedding. Then in goes a portable stove.

After fishing we drove back up to the cabin. We ate and then went into the tent and told stories and jokes. Everybody told something. I made up this story about Cheryl and Roger. Roger told about the ghost sled that helps people lost on the snow. This was all while sitting and lying on spruce branches while the little stove kept the tent positively tropical. It was wonderful.

— R.M.

To Adam and Janna Lewis,
Guelph, Ontario.
— R.M.

DOWN THE DRAIN!

Robert Munsch   Michael Martchenko

Adam jumped HIGHER and HIGHER and **HIGHER** and **HIGHER** on the trampoline.

"That's too high," said his little sister. "You're gonna get in trouble!"

"Am not," said Adam.

"Are too," said his little sister.

"Am not," said Adam.

"Are too," said his little sister.

Then Adam clanged into one side of the trampoline, flew across the yard and landed in the large pile of ashes from last week's marshmallow fire.

"ADAM!" yelled his father. "Your hands are dirty. Your face is dirty. Your feet are dirty. Adam, you need a bath!"

"No, no, no!" said Adam.

"Soap in my eyes!

"Soap in my ears!

"Soap in my mouth!

"I do not like baths!"

Adam ran into the kitchen, grabbed
the leg of the table and would not let go.

His little sister tickled his tummy.
Adam laughed and laughed and let go of
the table. His father picked him up, ran
to the bathroom and dropped Adam in
the bathtub, clothes and all.

Adam's dad turned on the
water and the tub started
to fill up.

Blub *Blub* **Blub** *Blub*
Blub
Blub **Blub**

Then the phone rang.
Ring! Ring! Ring! Ring! Ring!
"Stay right here, Adam," said his father. "Don't move. I'll be right back."

He ran down the hall, picked up the phone and said, "Hello? Hello? Hello? What's that? No money in the bank! But I can't talk right now, Adam is in the tub. Goodbye, goodbye, goodbye."

He hung up the phone, ran back to the bathroom, and was almost to the door when the phone rang again.
Ring! Ring! Ring! Ring! Ring!

He ran back down the hall, picked up the phone and said, "Hello? Hello? Hello? Grandma? Sorry, I can't talk right now. Adam is in the tub. Goodbye, goodbye, goodbye."

The phone rang again. He picked it up and said, "Hello? Hello? Hello? NO! Adam can't come and play. Adam is in the tub. Goodbye, goodbye, goodbye."

When Adam's father finally got back to the bathroom, there was water coming out the bottom of the door, the sides of the door and even the TOP of the door.

"Oh, dear," said Adam's father.

43

He opened the door really fast.

The whole bathroom was filled with water and Adam and his sister were swimming around inside.

Adam's father slammed the door before the water could get out.

He yelled, **"Adam! Pull the plug!"**

"Well," said Adam, "I might pull the plug if you got me a nice new skateboard."

So Adam's father went to the skateboard store and bought a nice new skateboard. Then he came back, opened the bathroom door really fast, threw in the skateboard before the water could get out, and slammed the door.

Then he yelled,

"Adam! Pull the plug!"

"Well," said Adam, "I might pull the plug if you got me a new pair of red running shoes, and a new dress for my sister."

So Adam's father ran to the mall and bought Adam a pair of red running shoes, and a dress for his little sister. Then he came back, opened the bathroom door really fast, threw in the shoes and dress before the water could get out, and slammed the door.

Then he yelled,

"Adam! Pull the plug!"

"Well," said Adam, "I might pull the plug if you got me an enormous hamburger."

So Adam's father drove to the hamburger store and bought an enormous hamburger for Adam. Then he came back, opened the bathroom door really fast, and threw in the hamburger before the water could get out.

Then he yelled really loud, **"Adam! Pull the plug!"**

So Adam swam down to the bottom of the bathroom and pulled the plug in the tub, and the water started to go around and around and down the drain.

Swish! Swish! Swish! Swish! Swish!

Adam said, "My skateboard and running shoes went down the drain!"

Swish! Swish! Swish! Swish! Swish!

Adam said, "My hamburger and my dog went down the drain!"

Swish! Swish! Swish! Swish! Swish!

Adam said, "My sister and the cat went down the drain!"

Swish! Swish! Swish! Swish! Swish!

"AHHHHHHHHHHHHHHHHHH!" yelled Adam. "I'm going down the drain!"

"Oh, no!" said Adam's father. He opened up the bathroom door and there was . . .

No water!

No hamburger!

No shoes!

No skateboard!

No dog!

No cat!

No sister!

And . . . no Adam!

Adam's father called down the drain, "Adam! Are you okay?"

From way down the drain Adam said, "Yes."

His father said, "Adam! Climb out."

"I can't climb out," said Adam. "It's too far."

"Ride your skateboard," said his dad.

"It's too slippery," said Adam.

"Put on your new running shoes," said his dad.

"I'm too weak," said Adam.

"Eat your hamburger," said his dad.

"WOW!" said Mrs. O'Dell.
"It is a great honour to be in a book."
Then she took everyone back to school, put the book on her desk, and went to tell the principal the wonderful news.

The book started to flip-flop up and down and say, **"Gwackh!"**

Ethan opened the book and said, "Hailey, are you OK? Do you still want to be in this book?"

"HELP!" yelled Hailey. "I am folded and scrunched and trapped and stuck, and I want to get out and go home."

"Don't worry," the class said. "We will get you out."

Rachel tried to scrape Hailey out of the book with a fingernail.

"AHHHHHHHHHHHH!" yelled Hailey. "That hurts!"

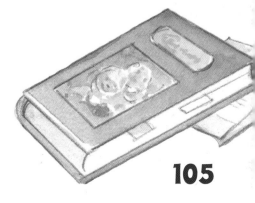

"I know what to do!" said Jakob. "We'll pull the book apart, and Hailey will fall out."
So a bunch of kids got on each side of the book, and they tried to pull it apart.

"AHHHHHHHHHHHHH!" yelled Hailey. "You're **STRETCHING** me!"

"Just twist the book and Hailey will pop right out," said Kiku.

They started to twist the book really hard.

"AHHHHHHHHHHHH!" yelled Hailey. "You're **SCRUNCHING** me!"

"This scraping and pulling and twisting are not working," the kids said. "We have to think of something different."

"Photocopy!" yelled Cole. "We can use the photocopy machine in the staff room and copy Hailey out of the book."

So everyone ran to the staff room and Cole tried to copy Hailey out of the book, but the machine only made pictures of Hailey. The real Hailey was still in the book.

"I know what to do!" said Laura. "We can squeeze her out of the book."

She put the book on the floor and everyone got on top.

For a while nothing happened. Then Hailey's nose sproinged out of the book. The book looked really strange with a nose.

AHHHHHHHHHHHH! yelled Hailey. "You're **squishing** me!"

The kids jumped off.

"Well," said Ethan, "at least the principal will be happy."

"And," said Cole, "Mrs. O'Dell LOVES having someone in her class in a book."

"But," said Kiku, "Hailey's mom and dad will not be happy that their kid is stuck in a book! How can you kiss someone goodnight when she is stuck in a book?"

"I've got it!" said Laura. "We can change the ending."

They ran back to the park, took the writer's marker, and wrote at the end of the book:

Then Hailey jumped out of the book and told the writer to find some other kid for his story.

"I don't understand," said the writer. "It is an honour to be in a book."

"RIGHT," said Hailey. She took the marker and wrote:

And then the writer wrote himself into the book. He could not get out and was stuck there FOREVER!

"AHHHHHHHHHHHHHHHHHHH!" yelled the writer from inside the book.

Jakob opened it and said, "Don't worry, it's an honour to be in a book."

Then Hailey gave the book to the librarian.

The librarian LOVED having a writer in the library.

And the book was very popular because it was the only one that bounced up and down on the shelf and yelled,

"HELP! HELP! HELP!"

121

Put Me in a Book!

A long time ago a girl named Dawn swam past my cottage and asked, "What if you put a kid in a book and the kid wanted out?"

That led to a story called Dawn's Book. Later I changed it into a school story that I would send out to classes that wrote to me. My secretary would insert the names of all the kids into the story. We started getting really nice books that classes made about the story.

Then we got THE BOOK.

A class from North Bay, Ontario, had done the story in REALLY NEAT PICTURES. It was wonderful and I immediately decided to make it the basis for my own book, and to use the kids' names from the class.

But when I went to look for the class, just a year later, I couldn't find them. The school had closed down! Luckily it turned out that the kids and their teacher had transferred to a brand new school nearby, and that is where I went to visit them to share my own version of their book.

— R.M.

*For Temina Girod,
Cold Lake, Alberta.*
— R.M.

The day before she went to see Grandma, Temina said, "Dolls! Dolls! Dolls! I can take all my dolls on the airplane."

"One!" said her mom. "You can bring just one doll."

"Pleeeeeeease," said Temina. "I will be very sad without ALL my dolls."

"One!" said her mom. "You can bring just one doll. You can't bring ALL your dolls. You must have 500 dolls."

"HA!" said Temina. "I have just 37 dolls. You know that I have just 37 dolls, not 500 dolls."

"One!" said Temina's mom. "You can bring just one doll."

"OK! OK! OK!" said Temina.

127

Then Temina said, "Toys! Toys! Toys! I can take my toys. I want to take all my toys!"

"One!" said her mom. "You can bring just one toy."

"Pleeeeeeease," said Temina. "I will be very sad without ALL my toys."

"One!" said her mom. "You can bring just one toy. You can't bring all your toys. You must have 500 toys."

"HA!" said Temina. "I have just 37 toys. You know that I have just 37 toys, not 500 toys."

"One!" said Temina's mom. "You can bring just one toy."

"OK! OK! OK!" said Temina.

129

So when Temina came to the airport, she was carrying ONE doll and ONE toy.

She was also carrying a backpack that had 20 dolls and 20 toys in it, but her mom did not know about those 20 dolls and 20 toys. Temina got her little sister to help her stomp and cram and squish the dolls and toys till they fit into the backpack.

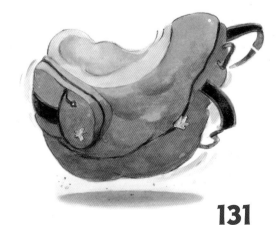

The backpack was very heavy, and Temina had trouble keeping up.

"Come on! Come on! Come on!" said her mom. "You are taking **FOREVER**. Let me carry your backpack."

"No!" said Temina. "MY backpack is MY backpack, and I will carry it!"

"Come on! Come on! Come on!" said her little sister. "You are taking **FOREVER.** Let me help you with your backpack."

"No!" said Temina. "MY backpack is MY backpack, and I will carry it!"

Finally they got in a long line.

A security officer said to Temina's mom, "Can I look in your backpack?"

"Yes," said Temina's mom.

Then he said to Temina's little sister, "Can I look in your backpack?"

"Yes," said her little sister.

Then he said to Temina, "Can I look in your backpack?"

"No!" said Temina. "You may NOT look in my backpack. My backpack is Top Secret."

"Right," said the officer. "How about we X-ray your backpack?"

"Well," said Temina, "You can do that, but do NOT tell my mom what is in it."

135

Then they walked and walked and walked and finally came to a huge skunk.

"How about a hug for my little brother?" said Thea.

"Hug?" said the skunk. "I love to give hugs."

And the skunk gave Tate a big skunk hug.

"How was that?" said Thea.

"Stink! Stink! Very yucky stink!" yelled Tate.

"OK!" said Thea. "Not a good hug."

Then they walked and walked and walked and finally came to a huge porcupine.

"How about a hug for my little brother?" said Thea.

"Hug?" said the porcupine. "I love to give hugs."

And the porcupine gave Tate
a big porcupine hug.
"How was that?" said Thea.

"Needles! Needles! Sharp poky needles!" yelled Tate.
"OK!" said Thea. "Not a good hug."

Then they walked and walked and walked and finally came to a huge gorilla.

"How about a hug for my little brother?" said Thea.

"Hug?" said the gorilla. "I love to give hugs."

And the gorilla gave Tate a big gorilla hug.

"How was that?" said Thea.

"Hard! Hard! Much too hard!" yelled Tate.

So Thea took her little brother's hand and they walked all the way back home.

Mommy said, "How was your walk?"

"Tate got hugged by a snail," said Thea.

"Slime! Slime! Lots of slime!" yelled Tate.

"And Tate got hugged by a skunk," said Thea.

"Stink! Stink! Very yucky stink!" yelled Tate.

"And Tate got hugged by a porcupine," said Thea.

"Needles! Needles! Sharp poky needles!" yelled Tate.

"And Tate got hugged by a gorilla," said Thea.

"Hard! Hard! Much too hard!" yelled Tate. "I need a Mommy hug."

So Mommy gave Tate a Mommy hug and Tate said, "Just right, just right, a just right hug."

"And the Thea who walked out the door so mad," said Mommy, "who hugged her?"

"Nobody," said Thea. "Nobody gave me a hug, and I am waiting for a Mommy hug."

So Mommy hugged Thea and Thea said, "Just right, just right, a just right hug."

And then they all had lunch.

Hugs

In March of 2001 I went on a ski trip to Sunshine Resort in Alberta, and I got a story idea in the restaurant during breakfast. I did not have a kid for the story, but I knew the name of one kid in the dining room because she was behind me in the buffet line, and I heard her mom say her name.

Once I was done with the story I went over to the family and found out that they live in Saskatoon, Saskatchewan. I told the parents what had happened and they were quite happy to have me tell the story to Thea and her little brother Tate, and that is how they got to be the kids in this story.

The parents took pictures of me telling the story and sent them to me later.

Hugs is my first book that was ever published as a board book first, although a lot of my books became board books after they were published as regular picture books.

—R.M.

How a Robert Munsch Book Is Made

Robert Munsch tells lots of amazing stories. But just how does one of those stories turn into a book?

The first step is to write the story down. Robert has been telling some of his stories for a long time, and they are a little different every time he tells them. He needs to decide which version to use in the book.

Robert sends the story, or manuscript, to his editor, who reads it and makes suggestions. Then Robert makes changes based on those ideas. They go back and forth like this until they feel that the manuscript is ready to become a book.

Once the story is finalized, it's time to work on the illustrations that will go with it. Illustrator Michael Martchenko and Robert Munsch have been a team for a long time — they have made more than 50 books together! They go to the publisher's office and meet with the book's editor and art director to share ideas about the story. They talk about what goes on each page and what the pictures might look like. Sometimes Robert will make changes to the story, and sometimes Michael will draw a quick cover sketch on the spot.

To help with the illustrations, Robert contacts the real kid the story is dedicated to, and gets permission to use that kid's

Michael and Bob brainstorming.

The photo of a Labrador tent that Michael used to create one of the paintings for *Give Me Back My Dad!*

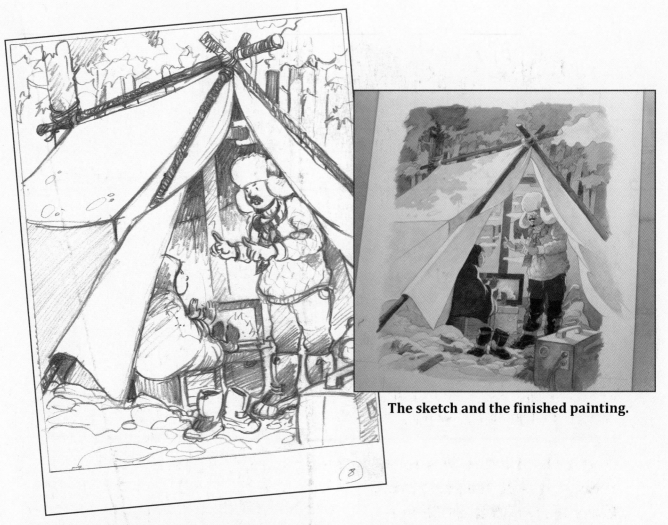

The sketch and the finished painting.

photograph as a basis for the character in the book. Sometimes he has photos of the kid's family, home and town to share, too.

When Michael has made pencil sketches for the whole book, there is another meeting. Michael spreads all the drawings out on a big table, and the editor, the art director and Robert talk about them. There are a lot of things to keep in mind: Do the people and places look the same on every page? Does what is happening in the drawings match the story? Are the pictures funny?

It can take several months to paint a book.

Sometimes Michael makes changes to the sketches, so he brings a big eraser with him. Once everyone is happy, Michael takes the sketches back to his studio and begins painting the final art.

Then the group gets together one last time. The paintings are spread out for everyone to admire. They laugh at all the crazy things Michael has painted and look for things he has hidden in the illustrations. (Here's a tip: look for a pterodactyl!)

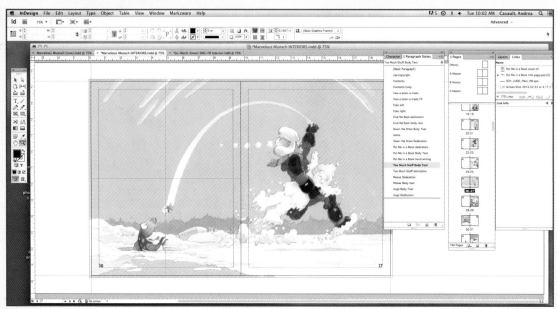

Now the book is in the hands of the art director. She designs the cover and the interior pages of the book. She puts the words and pictures together in a layout on her computer. She chooses fonts for the text and makes sure the colour is bright and correct, and that everything is in the right place. When she is done, Robert and his editor sit down together to give the story one last read and make final changes. A lot of the time they take some text out because an illustration shows a scene so well that no more description is required!

Finally the book is sent to the printer in Manitoba, where thousands and thousands of copies are printed and bound, ready to be sent to stores, libraries and schools across the country and around the world.